E
Evincepub
Publishing

Evincepub Publishing

Nehru Nagar, Bilaspur, Chhattisgarh 495001
First Published by Evincepub Publishing 2021
Copyright © Anindita Das 2021
All Rights Reserved.
ISBN: 978-93-5446-240-5

WHAT THE PANDEMIC LEARNED FROM ME

A hilarious antidote to the pain
that Corona dealt us

ANINDITA DAS

To the two men who have handwriting that puts mine to shame. And to the virus with great reluctance. Without it, I might not have felt brave enough to publish.

Statutory Warning

It feels like doomsday.

I spent my birthday alone at home, with 3 delivered cakes serving as proxy guests. Don't get me wrong. Though I am an introvert living happily with myself for probably a quarter of my life now, I still didn't see this coming. Birthdays earlier might have been equally boring, yet this one had a definite end-of-the-world feel to it. Suffice it to say that my friendless, pet-less, and guest-less Covid existence messed with my head enough to result in this debacle of a debut book.

Having said that, as we grapple with the second wave of Covid, enveloped in that knot of anxiety, delayed grief, and "doomsday feeling", one must find ways to cope.

Even in our most cocooned state of isolation, it's impossible to be unaffected and oblivious to the horrific images of tragedies happening outside hospitals, cremation grounds piling up with bodies, and the social media flooded with pleas for help. This book isn't a denial of the devastation that the virus has caused and the many lives that have been lost. In fact, I began writing this book in that season of delusion much before the second wave, when we all thought that we have beaten the curve and are well on our way to say, "remember Covid." But since we are back to tracking cases, I hope this book can ease some of the morose, the loneliness, the unpredictability, and ill-defined loss that is the "harsh now" and "maybe future" of our life.

I am eternally grateful to the concept of Work From Home that had no meaning in my life before the pandemic, perks of being in the advertising industry.

I am also grateful that the pandemic has brought on a surge of creativity in the lives of everyone. I now have many more friends turned influencers. I have also discovered newer positions of lying down on my two-seater without hurting my neck while worshipping OTT platforms. No mean feat.

A special mention to my clients who were in such a crisis mode that they never executed any of my approved campaigns. Thanks to their generosity, I had to find other ways to amuse myself.

Bottom line, I hope that this makes you smile a little bit. If not, you will get there one day.

About The Author

What do the world's most loved furniture brand, the nation's highest-selling mobiles and the highest on-time airlines in the country have in common?

They have all borrowed words from Anindita. Better known as Annie in the advertising circuits, she has also lent voice to hospitals, leading dailies, automobiles, fashion brands, FM channels, and gender-sensitive social causes alike. Her work has earned her several prestigious awards and accolades in creativity and effectiveness. An alumnus of the Indian Institute of Mass Communication, Delhi, she grew up with a love for storytelling in the green city of Guwahati. This is her first attempt to write something without a client's approval. She also giddily warns her readers that this isn't going to be her last book either.

Follow her on -

Website: authoranindita.com

Instagram: thisis.anindita

Facebook: thisisanindita

LinkedIn: thisisanindita

Contents

It's A Jungle Out There

Dear Plants,

Like everyone else imprisoned for an indefinite period in their not-so magical homes, I too had the urge to befriend you, little mean green things. I promise it wasn't solely because you would look so nice on my Instagram grid and that you were like adulting goals 101. Though I admit I am superficial like that, you being the closest thing I had to an obsessively adored pet or even to a living–breathing roommate. I loved you in my own selfish way and I hated it when you shamelessly hung out with other people, smiling from their balconies the morning after.

Despite my hopeless dreams of waking up one fine morning to discover a miraculously green balcony with many a flower smiling at me, our relation was at best a science experiment that I never understood, and you never reacted to. You lay there like an ingredient that in no way gives any clue whether it will explode or fizzle out, while I fumbled in the dark trying to balance impossible chemical equations.

All said and done, I will always remember each one of you and the way you alienated me during my pandemic gardening misadventure and serial murdering spree. Here are a few who survived my incessant mothering and coddling.

The Stubborn Snake Plant – I almost thought I had bought a faux plant by mistake. No amount of cajoling, cooing, rice water, plant food, or *jugaad* could make you snap out of your sulk. You looked exactly like the day you came into my life even after 6 months of nonstop selfless pampering – impoverished, unfriendly, stiff as a cardboard and in no mood to accept your new home. And here I was, sitting next to you and murmuring sweet nothings in the hopes of moving you to grow just a little bit.

The Money Plant On Mushrooms – I was told, you will tolerate even the worst kind of abuse, stay vehemently alive in water, soil, or that strange mystical material called cocopeat. While I had idyllic daydreams of you slowly taking over all my walls, dangling beautifully over my bohemian-looking headboard and my backyard railings (it has happened to people on Pinterest), the best you could do for me is slide off the top of the pot. But I do remember the lovely moment when you sprouted two new leaves, that's the most intimacy I ever shared with a plant.

The Fainting Aloe Vera – If suntan were a desirable thing in plants, you would have won all the beauty contests. I must blame the internet for telling me that aloe vera is a plant from dry desert area that needs little or no water. It's another matter that I decided to go with the latter option, and hence, the fainting spree. Once that began, no rock, stick, or any other support could convince you to look up.

The Jinxed Jade – I still remember the first time I discreetly made eyes at you, while you were sunning in the nursery in your adorable yellow polka-dotted planter. You had that air of someone who needed space and wouldn't mind me loving you from far. But never make the mistake of judging a plant by its planter. I was in for a bad surprise when you suddenly decided to die on me within a few days of our first meeting. Or was that your sinister plan all along?

The Moral Science Tulsi – *"Tulsi Maiyaa ko bas chod do, apne aap hi ugegi"* – Armed with this valuable management *gyan* by my magnificent *maali*, I strategically planned on fulfilling my gardening objective. But the three different times, I tried letting *Tulsi Maiyaa* be, the results were horribly same. Moral – Never take your *maali* literally. *Maiyaa* might get offended.

The Catch-Me-If-You-Coriander – You had my hopes high, that of me sprinkling you over a piping hot home-cooked meal and the room filling with your fresh aroma. If only. To give you credit, you did sprout, after I paid 10 times more for 10 grams of *Dhania* seeds, only to realize it's the same effing thing that we use for cooking every day. I kept waiting for the day you would fully (fully like the ones fertilized with growth hormones) grow, and I could sample you, not knowing that this was already the best you could do.

Despite the not-so-stupendous success of the first wave, the second wave of garden planning is well on its way. This upcoming jungle is also rumored to feature a Crazy Cosmic Cactus, a Brazen Bougainvillea, and a Fancy Fragrant Lily.

LETTER TWO

Mine Is Better Than Yours

Dear Social Media,

Lockdown or no lockdown, you are our savior from the little pockets of boredom that seem to erupt quite unceremoniously now and then, every 10 minutes in my case. You are like that frenemy who we hate and yet are addicted to. Especially when you are working from home for more than a year, you are like the only place we can look at, silently judging without being judged. Or maybe not so silently. After all, in the absence of any real social life (not that I had one before the lockdown), you are manna for our hour-long calls with our besties.

It never ceases to amaze me that no matter which floor you live in, which parks you walk in, and which place you come from, when it comes to you, everyone is playing the same game MIBTY – Mine Is Better Than Yours. Of course, there are many different versions of the game.

My Holiday Was More Foreign Than Yours – The more exotic and unheard of the foreign land is, the more charming the vacation is predicted to be. To make these near alien vacays happen, people will go to any lengths. Like climb a tree. Pet a tiger. Twist their bodies to look slimmer. Try life-threatening Mountain Dew–inspired sports. Dress like Yash Raj heroines in five-feet snow. Hire photographers and an entire entourage of BFFs. Make-up mind-boggling location tags. Trek for hundreds of miles even though back home they probably have never even walked down to their nearby ATM.

My Hobbies Are More Than Yours – Bread baking. Tie-Dying. Micro farming. Knife painting. Tik Toking. We are all masters of some fascinating new hobby or maybe a dozen.

My Plants Are Greener Than Yours – "In my house, my eucalyptus plant is all the room freshener I need." "My creeper grows so fast; I have to trim them more frequently than my underarm hair." "My greens are so green, even John Green would go green."

My Mental Health Is More Mental Than Yours – Not to sound insensitive (a tad bit difficult), but I mostly find myself utterly confused by pseudo-philosophical rants of people – the bottom line of which seems to be my grief is more than yours. My heart especially goes out to all those who end their status updates with, *"PS. Comments not solicited"* and yet refresh their phones every few seconds to check on all those who have paid no heed to their warning.

My Fitness Is More Fit Than Yours – Doing your crunches in front of the whole world is so much better than doing it quietly in your home. Especially, if you have not been able to step out to your gym thanks to the horrid virus.

My House Is Fancier Than Yours – Go to the farthest corner of the house. Angle your camera to get the best of the diagonal space. Throw in some pompoms and macramé art. You are all set.

My Life Is More Public Than Yours – You no longer meet people in parties. You no longer get introduced to friends of friends. So, you do the next better thing. You throw a party in your living room, in your bedroom, and in your closet.

My Talent Is More Talent Than Yours – Bachata. Skydiving. Baking. Painting. Like an endless conveyor belt, there are always more hidden talents to display. The worshippers of this cult are not humans, they are simply a lot of mind-boggling talent packed into a body of flesh and blood.

My Cause Is More Cause Than Yours – This game is played by everyone no matter how rich or poor. It's a niche version of the My Hobby is Better Than Yours and My World Needs More Saving Than Yours and usually has something to do with the planet, plastic, and poodles.

There's also MAIMA – My Advice Is More Advisory, MTIMTY – My Throwback Is More Than Yours, MHILTY - My Hashtag Is Longer Than Yours.

MLION – My Letter Is Over Now.

LETTER THREE

Work–Life Bla Bla Balance

Dear Work–Life Balance,

I have missed you. I missed talking about you mostly, mentioning subtly in those somewhat serious conversations that one has with acquaintances curious about the vicious advertising way of life. But honestly, we don't know each other so well, do we?

Ever since we stepped into the world of Work From Home, my day mostly begins at an ungodly hour in the morning (Post 9AM mostly) with a message from a particular servicing person who obviously is a morning person. Why? Because most certainly she needs confirmation for a meeting that is to be held the day after tomorrow, in the evening. Why would she even consider texting and take the chances of being ghosted? Why would she even think about waiting for normal agency office hours (agency being the keyword here) to begin.

If it's not her, it's my boss. He in his generosity has probably been waiting for an hour and counted till 100 before calling me with the day's agenda. He is most definitely a morning person. Once I am done with the call, while, still in my bed, a fleeting thought of starting my morning exercise passes my mind, though only for a second – because a crisis has already erupted on all the major WhatsApp groups.

Account Management 1 – *"The client has given some REWORK on the contest creative. It needs to go out TODAY and we NEED to start work ASAP! Please CONFIRM."*

I refuse to be riled up by the upper caps ruining my Zen morning routine, not dwelling too long on the pesky little fact that it does nothing for my mental health. I continue to stretch in my bed and ignore the message for two nanoseconds but more of them buzz like angry bees with even more upper caps. I declare enough is enough and send out a message missile of my own, *"Will check mail. Please WAIT!"* Seemingly harmless, it is saying a lot of things without saying anything like, *"Shut up, my day hasn't started yet. I will read the mail whenever I feel like. I will take my own sweet time to decide what I am going to do about it. In the rarest of rare cases (subject to the fact that you don't send me anymore messages), if I agree with the feedback,*

I might rewrite it. Otherwise, you will quietly go back to the client on your knees, plead, cajole, and do what you must till you make him see the light without the slightest hint on how to do so from me."

It doesn't matter that I have already gone through the mail twice in my sleep-induced state and parked it somewhere in the lower basement 2 of my priority list.

I move on to manage WhatsApp crisis 2, Junior 1 is absconding for the past 15 min, that's at least what Account Management 2 who has called her 6 times in the said 15 min is saying. You guessed it right, my junior is not a morning person either. But hysterical Account Management 2 needs my detective superpowers to find wherever my junior is at. I send some placatory messages and do nothing. Old age and years of futile proactiveness at work have taught me that showing harmless sedentary concern is the key to successfully tackle any crisis under the sun.

But hang on, Account Management 3 and my boss are asking me if I am joining the call. What call? I sit up straight on my bed and remove the gunk from the eyes. You are welcome, that's the least I can do for a client call. Not that it's a video call, we gave up on such niceties 20 days into the lockdown. I mute myself and let people assume I am mouthing the occasional *"yes"* and *"nice"* on mute, while I get to writing something that was due for this morning. The fact that it is a 9-page brochure that needs to be written in half an hour doesn't help. I argue that it is better to write it myself than to bet on Junior 3 who will probably mail it across after the deadline for me to rewrite it all over again. My furious typing is interrupted by someone mentioning my name on the call, asking me what I think of the two creative spaces. I want to say, *"some space would be nice"* but all I manage to say after rummaging my gob-smacked brain is that I would need to deep dive into it and get back later. Because quite frankly, the spaces had a seriously enviable talent of hiding inside miles and miles of fluff, faff, and buzzwords. There will be time enough to rip them apart later.

My meeting ends, and it is lunchtime. Just kidding! My boss is not into lunches, so he's fueled up to schedule meetings through the lunch hour. Though what happened to breakfast? Meanwhile, I hear Junior 1 has resurfaced and she vehemently disagrees that an Indian company should do a creative on International Day of Reflection on the 1994 Genocide against the Tutsi in Rwanda. While we are on the same page, I desperately need to get to the next page of my brochure. I also need to check what Junior 2 has been up to. The fact that I haven't heard him complain since the morning seems a little ominous. He needs to be in a perfectly agreeably naggy mood because a pitch brief bombshell must be dropped on his plate in the noon. But it is noon.

I join yet another call, pay attention for the first 5 min of the meeting, but then realize that 30 min have passed since it began, and during that time I have placed a Rs 5786/- Amazon order of which I can't recall a single item. Thankfully I regain consciousness in time to present my scripts. But the moment I turn my mic on, the food delivery guy decides to call. I disconnect and start presenting, now he is ringing my doorbell impatiently. I continue presenting on my phone, as I balance my delivery in my hands. My fake presentation smile turns into a grotesque grimace as I drop my food packets on the floor. The presentation does not go well.

The evening is a blur. I deeply regret not doing my laundry the previous Saturday and decide it must be postponed indefinitely or till I run out of clothes to dirty. I vaguely remember the HR calling me for the third time to finish my mandatory Mental Health Certification program. I log in and play the videos in the background and get all my answers wrong. I haggle with Account Management 2 to tell me the right answers and renegotiate a deadline in return.

The day is done, even the brief which came at 7.30PM has been sent out. Apart from cracking the campaign thought for the pitch, I have nothing to think of now. I decide the thinking will be played in the back of my mind like a Mozart lobby music. I sit back with a glass of hibiscus juice when outlook chimes. But of course, I forgot to fill my timesheet for 2 months and my salary is on hold. I doze off trying to remember how one was supposed to reach that darned thing called timesheet.

Skeletons In The Closet Collection

Dear Wardrobe,

Not long after we Marie Kondo-ed the shit out of our lives and sparked joy, we were hit by an exciting new phenomenon that we had so long adored from far. But IRL, we never dreamt that it could be happening to us anytime soon – Work From Home (at least not in Indian advertising agencies). We were catapulted into a hypnotic 24x7 pajama party that never ended once it began and effectively put you, our good old wardrobe to sleep for good.

And then something more happened, we realized we had overburdened you for way too long. With this realization, steps were taken, sometimes one too many. It was time to pull everything out, take stock of things, be overwhelmed into shock at how we had taken self-indulgence to another level, and finally, oscillate between a frenzy of activity and bouts of inactivity. All said and done, this routine happened not just once but several times in the past year. Wasn't that the point of calling it routine anyway? Every time, there was something new that blew our minds away.

Who knew nirvana was waiting for us, hidden buried under seven piles of clothes?

The Number Geek – Should it be just 33/3 (33 pieces of clothing for 3 months for the uninitiated)? Should it be a more liberal 100 pieces for all seasons? Or should it be 30 pieces for every season? How many pieces were too many? How many seasons should be considered? How many seasons are there though in our city? How many cities do I live in? How many times did I do my laundry?

The Crazy Capsule Creator – I will do my blacks, whites, and grays. I will add my neutrals and then there's my newfound love for beige to take care of. I will also throw in some statement pieces, to make a true capsule for a creative person. X must match Y, and Y must complement A, B, & C, which are dependent on how exactly X will be.

The Decluttering Demon – The favorite black dress from the season before. The trendy boot cut. The floral print puff sleeves. The compliment magnet satin skirt. Nothing can be shown any mercy. All hail the Decluttering Demon!

The Mostly Minimal Magician – Quality over

quantity. Clean classic cuts. No giving into this season's trends. No frills. No ruffles. Though wait a minute, does that mean nothing I currently own makes the cut?

The Window-Shopping Experimenter – Like Gandhi's experiments to test his celibacy vows, open every possible e-com site first thing after you open your eyes in the morning. Catch up on the new arrivals section. Drool, wish list, add to cart, feel giddy with excitement. Just don't buy anything.

The Sustainable Soul – Let fast fashion die a slow painful death. Thou shall not give in to their criminal marketing minds. Thou will only, live, breath, and wear sustainable indie brands. Thy love is pure, and thy responsibility is to mother earth above all else. Amen!

The Selfless Donating Devi – One for the house help. One for my friend's house help. One for the NGO. One for the recycling unit. One for the church. One for the ashram. One for Facebook. One for Twitter. Just let no one be bitter.

The Frugal Fashionista – Make a budget. Never exceed the said budget. Never lust after stuff that don't fit in real life. Stab your fantasy self and make peace with the fact that you will never be sitting at the Riviera in a backless red dress and 6-inch silver stilettoes. And never, never spend May's budget in January.

The skeletons came out again in spring and summer. Come autumn and the festivities, they might return to dance on the graves of the discarded.

LETTER FIVE

Vote for Vaccine

Dear Vaccine,

By vaccine, I am not being partial to a particular favored one. I mean all of you brethren from across the world, the miraculous species that has been the undying passion and immensely unhealthy obsession of an entire generation of people. Our relation has been a tumultuous one at best, oscillating constantly between manic hope and bottomless despair.

You were directly responsible for the improvement of general knowledge across various classes of people. Thanks to you, those of us who never had a newspaper subscription or even an app for that matter were now looking for news on your development every morning. No breakfast discussion or zoom call was complete without debating on the authenticity of the latest piece of news. It is safe to say this is the highest I have ever tried keeping up with news including the 9 months that I spent at the Indian Institute of Mass Communication. Yes, a 9-month course sounds strange and suggestive.

Rumor has it that you have successfully turned a huge chunk of atheists into a god-fearing lot praying specifically to the Patron Saint of Corona Controller. Then there were those who were now more diligent than ever to make up for their somewhat lax prayer routine. No wonder once the temple gates were thrown open to the public, each one of them felt the surge of a special superpower run through their veins and firmly believed that you were astoundingly going to descend on the despicable virus and strangle it to its fitting death.

And then, there were those who were scared shitless and have been living on a diet of unhealthy vaccine news. They are the kind of people who needed no demonstration in the aircraft that you are first supposed to wear your oxygen mask and then help others in times of emergency. They would do so anyway. They are the people who sanitize their gloved hands every 5 min and wear double masks every single day without feeling an iota of suffocation. They are the ones who were almost always the source of some good albeit fake news that the vaccine was ready, and they are the ones who were most heartbroken when it wasn't.

Then there were those who blamed the government for everything. Forget the vaccine, they denied the existence of corona itself. To them, it was yet another conspiracy to marginalize, oppress, and show the minorities in poor light.

Yet others believed it was the end of the world. So, vaccine or no vaccine made no difference whatsoever to anything. These apocalypse believers thought that their 10 minutes of Google search on the vaccine were naturally more reliable than the phony medical experts with an experience of several years of exploitation and their degrees earned after a number of years of education. No wonder they could never trust any of your kind, dear vaccine.

Special mention goes to those who needed a vaccine just so they could fly to their next vacation, to those who conjured all kinds of side-effect horrors, to those who delivered dark vaccine forwards at regular intervals, to those senior citizens who were happy they were seniors for the first time in their lives, and so on and so forth.

Surely, Certainly, Surprisingly

Dear Savings,

Since the time I was a neurotic kid obsessed with playing till I opted for the cheapest possible course in college, since the time I shopped every weekend at Sarojini till I eyed my first luxury bag, I never thought my aim in life would one day be to become a full-blown miser.

Not my father's well-meaning advice, my sister's borderline threats, my mother's Sherlock-like questions, "*Are you doing drugs? Where is your money going?*" or even my partner's ego-busting sarcastic jibes could reform me. This undoubtedly was the only thing in the whole wide world that didn't make me jealous of my friends. They could save all they want. In fact, once when a long-trusted astrologer advised my father that his youngest daughter would be very close-fisted with money, he really regretted consulting him for so many years. Surely and certainly, he was now convinced that he had wasted all the money that was used to consult the said astrologer so far, and for buying precious gemstones to align the pesky stars on his recommendation.

But then a million people (Just a hypothetical figure) lost their jobs, and it was a wake-up call for everyone on the planet to check their bank accounts. For many like me who had done nothing to nurture a robust relationship with you, it was like waking up with a bad migraine compounded by an urgent need to barf. However, desperate times needed desperate actions. And so, I set out on a journey to lure you into my life and in the course of time, I mastered quite a few things that might come handy to the ones who are financially handicapped like me. Here's an abridged version of the same in plain human language.

Luck Insurance Policy – This gamble is dark in theme. Firstly, you are either tempting your fate, daring to stay alive, in the hopes that if you are lucky enough to stay alive till you are old, you will still be in the mood to buy that Louis Vuitton bag or take that yacht cruise around the Spanish Riviera. Or worse, you are waiting for that certain someone you have nominated to try how to get away with murder.

Fixed Deceit Account – So here's money that you have earned to lock away in the deepest recesses of your mind, where you know that it's there, but it's certainly not. Until you can't remember where it began and where it ended, it's a whole new level of inception.

Recurring Damage Account – Little drops of water go on to make an ocean. Or so you have been told. But though these drops are such a drastically big dent on your monthly take home, you are nowhere near lying on a pile of coins like Uncle Scrooge. Admittedly, that's the only thing that seemed remotely attractive about you, my dear savings.

Retire-Meant Fund – A money pit that is idealistic and presumptuous like the Luck Insurance Policy especially in the times of Corona. It will tire you out slowly and steadily, and one day, when you least expect it, it will hurtle you down the stress-induced not-so-voluntary retirement path.

Systemic Illusion Policy – This is a more niche cousin of the *mutual funds sahi hai*. Though time will tell you they are one and the same, and both are equally capable of giving you a heart attack when you least expect it.

Public Painful Fund - It's a long-term relation where you lock in your money, hopes, dreams, and heart. And after you commit to this relation, if you find someone nicer which from my experience you will, it's simply your pain.

Mutual Fan Policy – It's like the truant child who doesn't believe in being sincere and hardworking. It's the kind of magic shortcut you were always looking for – that you think will turn your Rs 100 into a million real fast. Except this shortcut could take you nearly anywhere. *Sahi hai?*

On the other side of Corona, a great deal of these sordid schemes is awaiting to mature and bring about the much needed adulting joy in our lives. Till then, dear savings, you will remain that utterly seductive and genuinely impossible desire.

Starting Up 101

Dear Start-Up Ideas,

While this might anyway have been an era of having a business of your own, the pandemic did speed things up for quite a few people. And while everyone was having at it, I thought of no less than a few dozen of start-up ideas myself. Here's a breakup of the few that could be important to launch your glowing new business opportunity. All things considered.

A for App Developing. Think of something nobody needs. Then create a need for it using isolation as your excuse. Voila! You have the makings of a great app.

B for Bespoke Baking. When something is so sweet and pastel, it's bound to be a good business.

C for Chai Something. Or Coworking Something. Just get a big living room, blast the air conditioning, and save your Wi-Fi password as CHAI@654321.

D for DIY. Lamps, tables, notebooks, masks, umbrellas, handkerchiefs, fidget spinners, art, and disinfectants; just channel your craft classes and make something.

E for e-commerce. Much like the previous one, all you need to do in this case is to sell something.

F for Food Truck. Because food made inside a truck is fancier than any restaurant. Don your apron and why not give it a go.

G for Grocery Delivery. The desire to add groceries on to carts is inversely proportional to the graph of rising corona cases.

H for Homestay. When Daddy's got property, why shouldn't you prey. Just lead your communication with 7-level WHO-approved virus-free sanitization.

I for influencer. Step No. 1 Go shopping. Step No. 2 click some nice photos. Step No. 3 Make sure your friends and their friends like them.

J for Jewelry Maker. Qualifications required: either be a celebrity wife or have celebrity wives as friends.

K for Keto Foods. Because just-food is for the lame. To break into this niche, it would be advisable to dig deep into your Keto Salads.

L for Life Coach. Your own life is done for, so now you can successfully deal with that of others.

M for Microgreens. You obviously don't need too much space for this kind of a start-up. You can just start up.

N for Nightclub Promoter. Get all your friends to party at a place of your choice. Like a zoom call. It's as easy as that.

O for Organic Oxygen Farming. You have got to be part of the most *judagu* network ever. You also need to be savvy with getting celebrities to tweet all the information you want to share. Just don't forget to buy a pair of green rubber gloves and ensure that your packaging looks nice and green.

P for Podcasting. If you can speak, you can podcast. Pick the room with the maximum sunlight, some green plants in the background, a pro-looking mic and you are all set to wow the world with your verbal diarrhea.

Q for Quote Writer. Whatever you are thinking, just type, put the quotation marks, and share it on social media.

R for Reseller. Start small as a side hustle and grow it into a full-blown reselling business.

S for Solar Consultant. Basically, visit people's homes and tell them solar options for their homes.

T for Tours and Travels. Agreed that you can't really travel right now, thanks to Corona. But that's not stopping people from planning for the next trip with a vengeance. Maldives apparently is also going nowhere.

U for UI UX. Your client might know the whole shebang. The only thing he doesn't know is probably UI UX.

V for Vegan Everything. The world learnt their lesson from China. Well, at least, vegans did. Cash in on that.

W for Workshops. What the workshop is going to be on, that is something you can decide at a later stage, the important thing is to decide doing workshops.

X for X-rated. Saas Bahu Serials, Comics, Tik Tok Videos, Fiction, Punjabi Hip-Hop Songs. This market is always demanding more.

Y for YouTube Channel. Just find a niche (yes, that's important) and then shoot videos on whatever that is. Z for what? I haven't found that yet. Let me know when you do.

The Great Case of Grocery

Dear Grocery,

Never in my life I planned on becoming a nice, homely girl who knows how to pick a good bhindi from a not-so-good one by breaking off its tip at a roadside *thela wala*. Heartbreaking though it is, that's precisely what I have become.

At the ripe old age of 11 years, when my mother was traveling, I decided to make a solo entry into the kitchen with grand plans of mastering a mutton curry. It wasn't edible, which saintly though my father was, even he couldn't quite fathom its inexplicable taste and texture. That being said, I did beat my sister a few times in our impromptu lemonade and Maggi making competitions. She might not agree. But had anyone told me even at that high point of my life that one day I would become the queen of grocery buying, I would have completely laughed it off. I thought I was destined for greater things.

Come lockdown, everyone, including me, turned into these unreasonable hoarding monsters ready to suck anything into one of our many greedy gooey octopus-like claws. What we saw only in incredibly bizarre Hollywood movies where the world was always ending for one good reason or other, we were now seeing with open eyes in real life. Nobody knew how long the lockdown would last for, nobody knew how long before the home deliveries would resume, and how long the stores would remain closed. I had already mentally revisited the nightmare that demonetization was for poor people like me a thousand times. It involved standing outside a bank for 4 long hours only to withdraw Rs 2000 because that's what they were willing to let you and that's what your account anyway had at the end of the month.

So, I did what everyone else did, hoarded in anticipation. A situation I am not proud of but slightly better than hoarding oxygen cylinders. I bought stuff that I never ate in my entire life, namely, unnamables like *Dalia, Poha, Sooji, Rajma,* and Soya. In my head, I was picturing a day where I would be hungry enough to find these things eatable. Thankfully, that day never came in my life.

What came was even stranger. Now, my entire life revolved around your big business. In no time, I was shopping for what seemed like an entire Indian cricket team not just one single person who lived all by herself in an independent 2BHK.

I would patiently count my days, till the next grocery day. I would warn my maid exactly two and half times to not be late – twice during the week of the adventure, and once early morning on the day, with an impatient missed call. She made the mistake of being tone-deaf a couple of times; she had no idea what she was up against. So, while she busied herself with the chores, I had an early breakfast of just toast and butter because obviously who had the time for anything else. Then like a middle-aged uncle whose only validation in life is getting the family grocery, I would take out the neatly folded grocery bag, double-check my grocery list till I was 100% sure that I had indeed got it right, and happily set out for my quest.

I would patiently wait in the queue not minding the sun; I had already applied my dermatologist's recommended broad spectrum sunscreen for the special occasion.

While I waited, I would admire how every road looked different from the one outside my house, and how less traffic could make life so utterly beautiful. Once inside the departmental store, I was like a child in an amusement park, and all the withdrawal that I was feeling for not shopping anywhere else were to be taken care of here. I took my own sweet time going from aisle to aisle, waiting to discover those little gems that were perhaps not on my list, but which couldn't be ignored.

And at the end of it all, when I billed everything, the accomplishment I felt, I know many of you have felt that too.

Goa Wala Gaon

Dear Goa,

Even though we Indians have been treating you as nothing less than Las Vegas or Amsterdam since time immemorial, the Covid-19 situation entirely changed this whole game. Corona being the great leveler of people ensured that even the ones who would otherwise head to the distant Faroe Islands or the vibing beaches of Miami, now considered you as the mecca of fun times and pandemic permissible debauchery. The game now wasn't who wasn't visiting you, but for how long were they visiting you? And so, began the hunt for BNBs and holiday homes that afforded the visual luxury, the Work From Home tech requirements and the necessities of hygiene and safety. Because mind you, the more rigorous the safety and hygiene processes, the cooler the place seemed. The great metro populace who desperately wanted a break sought rental villas and cottages for long term of about 2–3 months and came with their families, helps, and pets in tow.

We fell in love with you with renewed vigor, celebrating the fact that you of all the places never judged us. It's why in the initial days, when you demanded no RT-PCR tests, all roads led to Goa. There was a sudden realization that made you seem blindingly better than living within the confines of the four walls of our now prison-like home. And though you always meant a lot of things to each one of us, you now meant a million more.

Content Calendar Goa – This Goa is exclusively for people who are more worried about the dwindling resources in their phone galleries than the current Covid statistics. Their only good intention is to add more masala to their timelines and followers to their profiles.

Mental Health Goa – This is strictly for the rich who can stay in nothing less than a heritage Portuguese Bungalow. They also need to preempt their mental health situation 3 months in advance to avail this rejuvenating option.

Dil Chahta Hai Goa – Clearly for millennials born much after the movie was released but they simply cannot help themselves when it comes to retro paraphernalia. Much like the Content Calendar Goa, this Goa is also about posing in Cabo De Rama and Chapora Fort.

Shoot At Site Goa – In the absence of any international shoot opportunities, all the scripts based in Corsica and Croatia have now been cut to good old Goa. This was slightly better than a budget revision because you could at least brag you were working on site and not remotely.

I Sleep Better In Goa – This is the Goa that belongs to insomniacs and true lovers of the place. Just knowing that they are in Goa is enough for them as they only come down here to catch up on sleep.

Private Plunge Pool Goa - In this Goa, the sun never sets, and the party never ends. Here, life isn't dependent on trivial curfew timings or the Section 144 on the beaches or even on the ban on communal resort swimming pools.

There's also the case of Maldives. But that's a different matter.

The Perfectly Fit Plan

Dear Fitness Plans,

You keep breezing in and out of our lives every single year, particularly around the time when resolutions are made only to be broken a few months later. But with the lockdown hitting our lives, most of us were more than happy to be reduced to slimy blobs of fat that existed quite frankly in a state of iceberg-like immobility. This, of course, was regularly rotated with our new fantasy version of our toned self, launched by the latest fitness fad. Add to that the baffling pandemic filter, and we found ourselves in the company of quite a few fitness avatars.

Like most people, my personal fitness routine during the pandemic comprised mainly of walks from the bed to the fridge and back. At one point, I was so motivated, I found my way up the stairs leading to the terrace where I proceeded to stare open-mouthed at the vistas my second-floor rooftop offered and ticked off a new milestone in my fitness journey.

Then began the frenzied evening walks. It started slow, with me trying to hit the 10,000 steps a day goal. It lasted for 2 long days.

I mostly daydreamt about working out a lot and hallucinated about reaching my goal of near-perfect midriff. Post achieving that flawless figure, I aimed to strut around confidently in nothing but crop tops without which there was anyway not much point to life. In due course, I learned the only way to reach this goal was to dabble with any of your following avatars. With so many options to reckon with, success couldn't be too far.

Workout In Progress – This particular fitness routine needs you to add a great number of online workouts to your Google calendar. Chances are the number of notifications you will get, will tire you out, and that itself will be a great workout.

Walk The Dog Regime – Lockdown has indirectly led to an era of astonishingly fit pets. This is a funny result of every member of the family walking the same dog at least once every day. While this might have some side effects on the poor traumatized pets, the owners have been known to be greatly benefitted. Possibly why everyone from Prince Harry to our very own Jonas *Jiju*, everyone is in this beautiful world with a beautiful dog.

Keeping Up With Keto – Not just the Kardashians, everyone is keeping up with keto. Case in point is the avalanche of keto restaurants cropping up all over. This diet works exceptionally well by throwing you into an overdrive of fat burning at a targeted part of your body – namely, your fingertips. Why? Browsing of food delivery apps!

Greenery Namaskar – If you have a balcony, you got to wake up early and arch your back for a Greenery Namaskar. While you are at it, make sure you capture this beauty along with the carpet grass and dangling creepers for your social media. The process is so therapeutic, it has been known to burn extra calories.

Branded Mommy Yoga – A certain actress Begum does a full spread photoshoot for a leading athleisure brand. This is enough encouragement to explode the ovaries of all expecting mommas who then go on to show off their own nice little baby bumps and start shedding the extra kilos even before the baby popped!

Phone A Friend Routine – This routine is a smarter multitasking cousin of the Watch Your Step Program known for impacting people from all walks of life. All you need for this to work is to find that one friend who always has an hour to kill every day. And then, while you are exercising your mouth, start walking to and fro.

Face Palm Yoga – This form of yoga doesn't need you to leave your seat. Nor do you need to reduce your screen time. You can also make various faces at your family members and completely get away with it.

Mental Meditation – This wishful fitness routine believes that a blank mind usually equals a blank appetite. Involving a lot of pastel scented candles, aromatic dark rooms, roomy pajamas, and chants from the gut, it is all about soothing your empty mind and the evil gnawing in your tummy.

The more determined ones are also trying a good permutation and combination of each of these routines. All the best to them!

Catch Me If You Can Cook

Dear Kitchen,

You have been the witness to way too many massacres this past year. As compared to the other years, when I would only step in to plate up my just delivered pizza or noodles, this was a completely different dough. We all rediscovered our inner Master Chefs within days of social distancing and blithely declared this to be the season of Banana Bread.

I personally ordered an OTG for trying out my baking skills after researching and reading a thousand and some reviews on amazon. I racked my brain trying to remember every little trick and tip my mother applied when she went about baking. I also browsed through a few and subscribed to another dozen channels on YouTube, all set to succeed on this gourmet mission.

In the end, my Banana Bread couldn't be differentiated much from a Boxing Bag. But dare I give up so soon, I almost immediately found the next mountain to scale or should I say recipe to conquer – sourdough. Meanwhile, a friend had announced on social media, *"Main bhi Nigella"*, while others doled our paellas, bruschettas, quesadillas, risottos, baklavas, truffles, and other fancy-sounding food in vengeance. There was serious catching up to play. I labored on tirelessly, weekend after weekend, cooking meals after meals, only to realize every single time that there was no one coming over and it was me who is doomed to finish all this food.

When the baking spree was done with, it was microgreens. Another friend's kitchen garden was flourishing while mine was dying a slow painful death. Then there was the time of rustic village-style cooking spree done in earthenware clay pots.

All said and done after bravely weathering these unpredictable cooking seasons, I now have some valuable lessons in life, which I am more than ready to pass on to the next generation.

1. There's no need to make a five-course meal, Queen Elizabeth is hardly going to visit you during the lockdown.

2. You do need to peel off the skin of that green vegetable that looks like a pear but isn't.

3. You do need to peel off the skin of an apple, because it has been coated with wax to look like a shiny showpiece.

4. There are more kitchen herbs than *dhania* and *curry patta*. Like basil, thyme, rosemary, dill, oregano, all of which you don't need to grow.

5. *Tur daal* and *maa ki daal* are basically same but not really. Also, the latter isn't a real swear word, it's your mind that's dirty.

6. It's possible to eat brown bread even though it is of the same disgusting color as that unnamable thing.

7. It's better to have breakfast in the morning than in the evening.

8. Plating is everything, it can even make unappetizing *ghiya* tolerable.

9. Branding is everything. What? Don't you have your own *masala korma peanut butter Maggi trademark?*

10. Practice does not always make perfect. No matter how much *poha* you eat, you never reach that point where you finally begin to enjoy it.

11. The *bharwa* version of everything is like the premium exclusive ultra of everything. Like *Bharwa Baigan, Bharwa Bhindi, Bharwa Karela, Bharwa Mushrooms, Bharwa Chicken, and* so on and so forth.

LETTER TWELVE

Oh My Virus

Dear Viruses,

While the world had gotten up and taken notice of the leading virus of our lives, there were plenty of you, other lesser viruses that are spreading just as fast. These though not life-threatening have wreaked rampant havoc all around. I thought it was my duty to bring everyone's notice to these, if for nothing else but to acknowledge the fact that I see what you are doing here.

Chinchinditis: A condition of acute confusion regarding where one should wear one's mask. Spreads from colony to colony through a process known as *"other people are also doing this."* Has been known to be fatal.

Vipflu: This infection makes the patient believe that if you are a VIP, you are entitled to fly off to a certain blue water haven. Typical symptoms include indifference, insensitivity, and lack of compassion. However, most patients have been known to be asymptomatic.

Briberia: An infection in which the patient tries to grease palms whenever caught without a mask. The virus is known to spread from hand to hand and cause severe pain in the pocket.

Hairypox: Lockdown resulted in a great number of patients assuming that just because you are looking the other way and closing your eyes, no one else can see your body hair too. If not treated on time, this infection can lead to **Animalitis** and **Self-Haterohea.**

Curfewbitis: A dyslexic disease that does not allow the infected person to stay indoors after the curfew hours. Patient feels compelled to break curfew, gather in crowds, and wait unwearyingly all the while tempting fate.

Redlitis: Patients suffer from a scant lockdown traffic hangover and expect it to last forever. Other symptoms include inability to see traffic for what it really is combined with acute vision and memory loss. Infected people also believe that if four cars approach a crossing and the red light is not working, there is no need to pull the brakes, they only need to close their eyes and drive on.

Evasionia: Known to attack patients in power hot seats at their most vulnerable – during a press conference or while addressing the public. In this mental delirium, patients go into a trance like state with an unshakeable belief that others can't see through their nonsense while they continue to mumble unrelated incoherent nonsense.

Pavementaria: The spread of the idiotic notion that just because you are standing on the pavement right outside your home, you are immune to everything. Patients show symptoms of extreme narcissism that lead them to believe that they can run indoors anytime if the greater virus shows up at their doorstep.

Abormalia: Much like Evasionia, this virus takes a grip on the patient's mental faculties, making them give up on whatever is normal. Infected patient also shows signs of utter lack of emotion, doesn't struggle in accepting bizarre life situations, and dismisses everything with an excuse of it being, what else – new normal.

Though unwanted, the second wave and the post-pandemic world might bring about a new wave of viruses. One can only hope not to be bitten by those. Fingers crossed; I say.

Book The Title

Dear Books,

Without you, life would be a great deal duller, relationship goals more realistic, and disappointments a tad bit less hurting. Still, what would this real world even be worth if there was nothing loftier to compare it to. You have been every bookworm's (even though our population is dwindling at a rapid speed next only to the vile virus) solace and stay while we were cast away into the vagaries of lockdown. A predicament no lesser than the ravages of the World Wars or the Bubonic Plague of the middle ages.

That brings me to the little question, if I was not writing this book, what would I be writing or for that matter, all the writers worth anything writing. While one could write any number of things using what we call our fertile imagination, it's best to do some prior research. So, here's a ready reckoner on all the mega magnetic plots that can catapult anyone's career into that of a bestselling, royalty collecting, TED Talk giving, autograph signing author of repute.

Love In The Times of Corona – The book of balcony romance and lovers separated by the great mean lockdown. In a major twist, throw in a death or two of the favorite characters, a video call or four, and resurrect the resilience of human spirit. You are more than ready to sign a major motion picture deal.

The Vaccine Thief – Vaccine is the only hope in a world that is dying. A mysterious central character untouched by the grief and trauma induced by the macabre mutating virus goes about stealing one thing that can save the human race. What is his secret motive? Will the best minds of the world be able to unravel him? How will his journey end?

The Virus Code – A mystery thriller featuring the ruling government, the medical scientists, and the vaccine mafia. Together they guard a volatile secret about the virus, aboriginally hidden 2000 years ago in a painting we all love.

Fifty Shades Of Corona – What better time for erotica than the many waves of shuddering lockdown. In it, together are two sex-starved fabulous-looking characters who are stuck in isolation in nothing less than a shiny penthouse.

Throw in some scintillating positions, a childhood trauma here and there, and you have a winner in your hands.

Gone With The Cylinder – A love story with a difference. Our heroine is a manipulative woman in love with a roguish hero. Destiny pits them against each other many times, until their love faces one final test - they are left with the last oxygen cylinder in the world. To survive, only one of them can have it.

Eat Pray Leave – A single person's life-affirming tale of self-discovery and survival. From Maldives to the Caribbean, this person's journey out of her comfort zone in the times of the pandemic is just the healthy dose of pink fluff every reader need.

To Kill A Mocking Virus – This is a grappling account of the migrants severely hit by the pandemic and their desperate attempts to get a grip on their new reality. Together, they devise a plan to take on the Goliath Virus. Will they win this battle?

The Lord Of All Vaccines – The future of the mankind is tied to the fate of one antidote lost to the civilizations. In a battle of wits and strength, powerful forces unleash a relentless search for the antidote. Who holds the key to this antidote?

Memoirs Of Coruna – Narrated by a street worker in Kamathipura, this is a graphic retelling of the residents of the area during the pandemic. Despite the uncertainty of the virus, struggles of isolation, and personal tragedies, how does each of the characters develop and discover meaning in their lives.

New plots seem to be developing every hour since the second wave hit us. But the bigger plot rests on what the virus has planned for us. Only time will tell, what that's going to be.

Fancy New Freedom

Dear Freedom,

Many of our ancestors fought for years, giving up on love, family, and career, so that future generations like us could make the most of you. And boy, did we? Then one fine day, life dealt a hard slap across our faces and now, we don't know for sure what you were meant to be. Even the smallest of things that gave us a little happiness led to an emotional meltdown of the next level. While we vented and ranted about the quarantine life hoping to wake up miraculously from this dystopian nightmare, we also discovered a newfound respect for the life that was, that we had left behind.

Though we didn't realize it yet, our new life too had many unexpected hidden blessings. Big or small, strange, or common, they did make our lives so much more livable while we were at it. Here are a few obvious charmers.

Freedom To Diffuse – Put away your expensive perfumes and erotically advertised deodorants for the next life. In this pandemic life, you can bask in the stench of your body odor and shine in the highlighter of your sweat, diffusing guilt-free stink.

Freedom To Burp – Not that this freedom did not exist earlier, but now more than ever were we truly enjoying the marvels of our kitchen and the food delivery apps. So, what if few of us weren't comfortable heading out to a restaurant yet, we were absolutely okay digging into something that's strictly forbidden by dieticians.

Freedom To Hot Pants – The best mishaps on video calls capture butts dressed in a variety of colors. These mishaps aside, you are now free to roam around your house in whatever catches your fancy all day long. You can also run out of the shower in your birthday suit while your partner is on a promotion propelling teams call.

Freedom To Balcony – Or may be a window if you don't have a balcony. Sit there quietly, peer into the world with your tiny judging eyes. Play some mean commentary in your head. The joy will be pure gold, comparable only to the feeling you get while stalking people on social media.

Freedom To Unibrow – Gone are the days of

wasting hard-earned money just because the parlor aunty thinks your skin is looking worse or your hair is drier than last week. All hail the unibrow! It's time to be a hairy fairy or a hairy knight (Insert the picture of certain bare-bodied hairy hero of yesteryears here) if you might. There's no one judging you because obviously, there's no one.

Freedom To Gargle – You cannot control tragedy and loss, but you can control the number of times you gargle in a day. As you gargle and steam out of this mess, you will find a direction not just from the nose to your gut but to the secrets of this wonderful life itself.

Freedom To Drunk – What's the best thing you can do if you can't go out and party? Party at home of course. Doesn't matter that you have got to stand in a queue flouting all norms of social distancing outside the *theka* longer than you ever did outside *Sulabh Shauchalaya.*

Freedom To Marinate – In your head silly. Think about all that was and all that could be. Think about the loved ones you lost touch with. Think about the connections you will renew. Think about every joy you let go off, every laughing moment you didn't have time to savor, every opportunity for fun and adventure missed. And with that renew the determination to wait this dark period out till you can reclaim this god-dammed beautiful life.

Freedom To Stress – If someone's stressing you out with stories of *"my stress is more than yours,"* feel free to give them a dose of your stress. Share a horrifying video, an alarming new forward, a tragedy experienced by someone you know of. Guaranteed to shut them up and show great results for your well-being.

So, the next time everything feels a little too gloomy, pause for a moment and think. What's the one freedom you are going to exercise the next?

Jump The Boards

Dear School Days,

So far, I only ever had a scant few complaints about you, but what you are now doing in collaboration with the virus is something we have to talk about. We, the ones who grew up, spent our school days waiting endlessly for that once-in-a-blue-moon rainy day when our mothers would deem fit to say that it was okay to stay back at home. We hoped against hope that *bandhs* that were passed even by the most obscure organizations would be strictly enforced, and the school bus wouldn't come to pick us up. On rare days, when a VIP passed away, and a bandh was declared, there was no limit to our jubilation.

Like everything else, joy was delivered in small frugal portions to be savored cautiously without feeling too happy, for fear that it might be taken away. Compared to that, school life in these unparalleled times is an anomaly, an alien transgression of sorts. Who would have thought attending classes online that too for an entire year would one day become a new norm?

Then comes exams, the nightmare of the backbenchers, and orgasm of the toppers. If exams were suspended even once during my student life, I am absolutely confident I would have done exceptionally well in life. I mean like young-rich-jet-setting-globetrotting-CEO-kind-of-well, I think. But we never had that kind of good fortune, did we now?

School life was a dreadful build-up culminating in one allegedly major life-altering event – your boards. It is at the altar of this divine year that we sacrificed our childhood and teenage years. Preparations began well in advance, particularly if your parents are the strategic types. From procuring notes of a meritorious senior to all kinds of experimental coaching to constant comparisons with illustrious single-minded siblings to discipline shaming, you are subjected to a multitude of third-degree torture techniques. But imagine being a pre-boarder in the current scenario and suddenly getting the unbelievably good news that your nightmare no longer exists. You are amongst God's chosen few who will not be judged based on what you score. Your victory is the victory of an entire generation of students, and indirectly, that of our questionable education system. For once CBSE, ICSE, and the state boards all deserve to make the most of this mind-blowing marvel in a student's life.

One cannot help but feel a little envious of the current crop of students who are living these fantasy lives absolved of all the terrors of an average student's life. This is precisely what was lacking in my school days (apart from 4G-enabled smartphones to seek answers and demand exam cancellations) freedom to learn as one pleases without the fear of marksheets and exams lurking at every corner.

Virus or no virus, I must admit, albeit reluctantly that, this is the perfect time to be a school-going student. Sure, going to class and having actual face-to-face interactions with friends is something that can never be replaced, but the charm of skipping an exam is incomparably attractive.

LETTER SIXEEN

An Apology of a Farewell

Dear Departed,

There's possibly no easy way to come to terms with what happened and write this. Almost all of us have had to say goodbyes far too soon to someone who was our whole world, someone we loved or someone we knew or someone we lost touch with or someone we heard of. While the grief may not be same in each case, this feeling of suppressed anger, vague restlessness, bleak uncertainty, and emotional fatigue is real for each one of us breathing today. We, as a world are grieving together.

Many of us who may have protected ourselves long from all the distressing news and information that enveloped us from every direction since the beginning of this global catastrophe have finally given up on this extremely sad and equally unsustainable bubble. There's no more denying the world that we live in, a world where every hour is worse than the one before, where oxygen is the currency of the times, black markets and frauds are rampant everywhere. The medical fraternity is fatigued beyond human limits. The hospital beds are not enough, and an abysmally huge number of patients are dying all at once due to this acute shortage. Social media has become a place for churning out SOS and obituaries. Parks and parking areas are being turned into crematoriums overnight. The capital has run out of firewood for cremations and the Forest Department has had to direct the Delhi Government to fell trees to compensate the deficit – bringing the world to a full circle.

In the words of Arundhati Roy, *"We speak to those we love in tears, and with trepidation, not knowing if we will ever see each other again. We write, we work, not knowing if we will live to finish what we started. Not knowing what horror and humiliation awaits us. The indignity of it all. That is what breaks us."*

Each time we get bad news, we are tossed into an ocean of guilt, wondering if there was something we could have done. Regretting, not making that call, not making time for important occasions. Then incessantly worrying about those that remain behind, wondering how much time we are left with together.

There is no changing the fact that you have passed over; and it is high time we own up to our mistakes, give you the apology you deserve. For every time we thought it was okay to let our guard down for just a little bit. We reasoned what harm could happen in a matter of minutes? For stepping out all those times when we could have stayed home. For not missing any birthday, wedding, party, rally, tournament, meeting, road trip, and everything happening this side of the world. All because we could not bear being stuck inside our homes anymore. For taking a mask break because we couldn't take the nausea.

For not taking a test even when we were showing all the symptoms and endangering you, simply because we were too scared. For not letting all who we met know that we were positive and let them prepare for what's might be coming. Then again stepping out too soon without even a negative report in our hands, just because we felt alright. For the fake negative reports, we sold and bought because we as a country somehow did not want to do any better even when our lives were at stake. For the oxygen, we hoarded hidden in our homes not thinking of you who needed it more.

For not questioning enough when we were asked to get back to work too soon. We accepted coming back home defeated every day while exposing those waiting for us at home to unnecessary risks. We continue to do so unable to decide whether the virus or fear of hunger is bigger.

For letting our pointless pride stop us from speaking our mind when we needed to stop you from being careless. For leaving you alone to fend for yourself when you were unable to ask for help. For being a cynic and nothing else. For failing you, you who had come many miles away from home in search of livelihood and a life of dignity, only to be thwarted away, migrating back on foot, hungry and parched. For not letting your ambulance pass on the road and distressing you even in your last hours. For being filled with doubt about how things are being run in this nation but being too lazy to do anything about it.

This apology may not mean anything at all to you now that you are free of this human life. But even now, this isn't about you. We must assuage our guilty selfish conscience, so we are able to sleep peacefully at night, and hope that the message is delivered. And even though it's the virus that killed you, we killed you a little too by our dangerous indifference, disgusting insensitivity, and callous carelessness. We never deserved you.

Punjabi Beat Ve

Dear Punjabi Songs,

No matter how bleak things are today, one thing is certainly coming our way tomorrow. Like it or not, there's no escape from Punjabi songs, whether the Bollywood ones or otherwise. We will soon reach a point where we will be remixing them in our head and start belting our improvised similar-sounding versions of what the actual songs are. But before we reach that stage, it will be wise to quickly take stock of the immense possibilities.

No point blaming the writers later and complaining that gone are the days of actual emotion-stirring poetry and lyricism that stayed with you forever. All that can wait, but first a very heavy dose of pulsating titillating mind-numbing Punjabi tracks. Why? Because frankly that's one of the best things we can listen to, to get our minds off toxic corona times, and bounce back on the track of serious, and persistent positivity. Nothing else will do.

So, without further faff, here's a list of my possible top 10 songs that's highly likely to enter your playlist very soon.

1. **Main Tera Vaccine, Tu Meri Virus...** Oh Menu Kehndi Na Na Na... you know how it will go after that.
2. **Tenu Mask Suit Suit Karda...** Sing a compliment, keep bae safe. Honestly, what else matters?
3. **Sadi Gali Virus Na Laya Karo...** Sanitizer se roz nahaya karo, vaccine har haal lagwaya karo, the options are plenty.
4. **Lockdown Lockdown Kendi Rehti Ei Kudi...** She won't jump the curfew; she's got some style.
5. **Fever Si Chad Gayi Oye...** Bring down the soaring temperature with a good shake of the booty.
6. **Ho Jayegi Covid Ho Re Ho Jayegi...** A veiled threat is the best way to convince people, isn't it?
7. **Oxygen Dena Oxygen Lena Sauda Kara Kara...** Business is business, and this is now everybody's business.
8. **Virus Hawa De Vich Bikhar Gaya...** Not so Mauja Hi Mauja. Meet the airborne disaster with a high-frequency number.
9. **Vaccine Da Rang Dekhke...** Who wouldn't get emotional on getting vaccinated?

10. **Chuck De Chuck De India...** The virus is
going to dread the day when all of Delhi
and Punjab chants this way.

Personally, I never thought I would live to see the day when I would demand a Punjabi song from a deejay, but I guess the time is ripe for it. All the people who have seen my schizophrenic self on the dance floor, know what might happen soon. The only question that remains is when that party will be a legit possibility.

Hang On Till Tomorrow

Dear Tomorrow,

I intend to live.

I plan to catch up with you on the other side of this story with the same obnoxious enthusiasm that people had for Dalgona coffee sometime back. I will no longer dwell on the fact that you may still be as uncertain and sly as you were yesterday. I no longer care what you have in store for me when I finally meet you. All I know is that I simply refuse to be ousted by a pesky insidious virus. It will take more than that to bring me down.

So, when I meet you on the other side of this mayhem, I mostly want to forget about the horrors that I see all around me today. Forget all about the gnawing fear that never quite subsides. Forget the brutal realization of our inevitable mortality. But there are a few things we will probably have to remember for the sake of our collective sanity.

This here's a quick list that we can pack into our mental rucksack and carry along to tomorrow when we finally say goodbye to blasted corona.

#1. If you are planning to call and check on someone, don't wait for tomorrow. Tomorrow is going to have the exact same 24 hours as today. Studies also shows that the effort it takes today to pick up the phone and dial that number, will be exactly same tomorrow.

#2. Personal hygiene is something that needs to be maintained every day. No point having a massive sanitizer spa day today and ignoring it for the rest of the week. That hasn't worked out well for anyone.

#3. Distractions are magical. Especially the kinds you call hobbies. They take your mind off all the inescapable toxicity and make you feel like there's so much more to life than just paying credit card installments before due dates.

#4. Plans need to be made. Vacation plans. Job switch plans. Shopping plans. Promotion plans. Investment plans. Family plans. Because plans are like small packets of 'hope' that you can pop in anytime to get you through everything bland that life tosses your way.

#5. Humans can be evil. Our continuous exploitation of natural resources and destruction of animal habitats have made us closer neighbors to them, and this proximity has led to catching infections from them faster. In other crude words, we should never forget that we have somehow brought this all on ourselves.

#6. Humans can heal. Simply by amplifying a message. Simply by calling and checking. Simply by getting information. Simply by collecting a cylinder. Simply by getting someone food. Simply by a little kindness. Simply by being humane.

#7. Everything you need to keep going is within you. All you have to do is know how to reach within and grab hold of what you need by its collar and yank it out with unshakeable determination. It also involves looking into the mirror and giving yourself pep talks in the middle of the night.

#8. You don't really need much to be happy. A nice window, a Netflix connection, a few good books, and a loaded pantry mostly does the trick. A couple of genuine friends, a well-bruised passport, a few Instagram stalkers, and an imaginary pet couldn't hurt either.

#9. Some journeys are best made by yourself. If you have the support of your dear ones, it's great. If not, they are only busy playing catch up.

#10. Life is best gulped in small doses. Even though there are the ones who have been telling us to plan for our future, at times 5 years ahead, it is best to just hang on till tomorrow. Don't stress so much about what you can't control or change. This situation is teaching us that we can find peace even if circumstances are beyond our control. The mystery and suspense that comes along are just extra bonus.

With this I leap forward to tomorrow. To all who have read this and those who haven't yet, I only have one advice. Please live. Ferociously. Adamantly. Cheerfully. I am counting on it.

www.ingramcontent.com/pod-product-compliance
Lightning Source LLC
La Vergne TN
LVHW041713190726
843493LV00007B/2073